SACRIFICE

SACRIFICE

A FALL FOR ME PREQUEL

K. A. LAST

www.kalastbooks.com.au

K. A. Last
kalast@kalastbooks.com.au
www.kalastbooks.com.au

ISBN: 9780987384935 (paperback)

Book and cover design by KILA Designs | www.kiladesigns.com.au

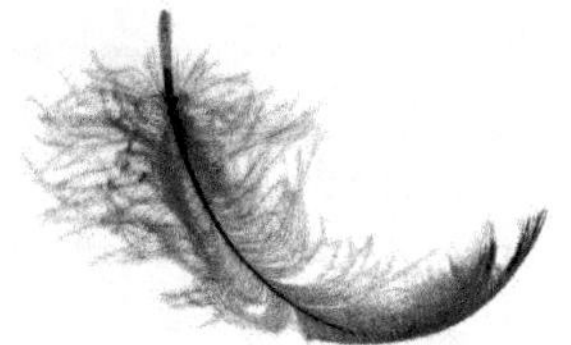

For Brendon; the one who makes
all the sacrifices for me.

Love is a smoke rais'd with the fume of sighs;
Being purg'd, a fire sparkling in lovers' eyes;
Being vex'd, a sea nourish'd with lovers' tears;
What is it else? a madness most discreet,
A choking gall, and a preserving sweet.
William Shakespeare – Romeo & Juliet, Act I, Scene I

PART ONE
SETH

1642

M ichael and I had been fighting for almost an hour. Cloud dust plumed into the air as my feet struck the floor. My patience with him was growing thin. He couldn't say anything that would change my mind. As far as I was concerned he was wasting his time.

"You can't do it," Michael said. "You don't know what you're giving up."

"I know perfectly well what I'm giving up," I said through clenched teeth.

"But why, Seth? Why leave when you can be with her every day?"

"Because I can't *be* with her, can I? It's against the rules."

"It has to be better than what you're planning. Imagine if she knew."

"She won't find out until I'm gone," I shouted. "No one will find out. And if you tell anyone I'll—"

"What?" Michael folded his arms over his chest. "Kill me? Hit me? What, Seth? What could you possibly do to me? I'm an archangel. I'm your superior, and as your superior, I'm telling you not to do this. Actually, I'm ordering you not to do this. Don't think you can get anything past the Council."

Michael stared at me with heavenly wrath in his eyes. My shoulders heaved as I tried—unsuccessfully—to contain my anger. I lunged at Michael and hit him in the chest. He stumbled backwards then righted himself and unfurled his pearl-white wings to their full span. He came at me with a force ten times stronger than my own, and I landed heavily on my back in the cloud dust.

"Grow up. Stop thinking about yourself for once; think about what this will do to her. It will crush her."

Michael pinned me to the floor. I struggled beneath him, but he held me firmly in place.

"Get. Off. Me," I said.

Finally, he did as I'd asked. I sat up, ran a hand through my hair, and watched Michael walk away. He kicked at the cloud dust as he went. The mist floated before settling back into place.

"You don't understand," I said. "I *have* thought about this. I've thought about it until my head feels like it's going to split open. I love her."

Michael turned to face me. "Then why is being beside her not enough?"

"There's no room up here for her *and* my heart. Because when I'm with her, I want to break every vow I've ever made. And I can't ask her to do the same."

"Then I guess we've got a problem."

I got to my feet and squared my shoulders. "Yes, I guess we do."

2

Our gazes met across the expanse of white. She smiled and it touched her eyes. Her face lit up as if the sun was shining from within her, making her skin glow.

Grace was the most beautiful angel I'd ever seen.

For a few moments I stood like a complete dolt staring at her. Then the cloud dust exploded and obscured Grace from view.

When the dust settled, Michael stood before me. He looked down his nose, shook his head and laughed. A wide grin spread across his mischievous face. He stretched his wings and they lifted him into the air where he hovered in front of me. He was still pissed at me and trying to exude his importance.

"Do you always need to make such a dramatic entrance?" I asked.

Michael laughed again and shrugged. "You know me.

Someone needs to keep it light around here. Everyone is far too serious."

I flapped my wings and rose to Michael's level. There was no way I was going to let him get the better of me. We continued up until the other angels were out of earshot.

"That's not the impression you gave me this morning. Besides, serious is what gets the job done," I said.

Michael shook his head. "What's happened to you? You used to be so … I can't believe you're doing this."

I sighed. I wasn't in the mood for another argument, and I knew why he'd come, so I changed the subject. "What do they need this time?"

"Hey, I'm just the messenger," he said, putting his hands up. "Don't shoot me. You have to take it up with them."

Yes, I'd have to take it up with them. My next mission was something I'd been waiting for, but now I wasn't sure if I should go. If I did, it meant I would finally have the chance to follow through with my decision. But the thought of leaving Grace made me feel sick.

Michael and I floated down until our feet rested in the cloud dust. I looked over his shoulder at Grace and she grinned. She also knew why Michael had made an appearance. He'd become predictable with his showy entrances to the cloud field—the place the angels rested before their next summons or duty.

It's time again? Grace asked.

I nodded slightly so she knew I'd heard her, but I didn't reply. Angels can talk to each other silently. All I had to do was think what I wanted to say and she'd hear it in her head, but I didn't really need words when I was near Grace. We'd been friends for so long we were completely in sync, like we were a part of each other.

The angel beside Grace raised her head and furrowed her brow. Angelica and I very rarely saw eye to eye. She was on a higher level, and her job was far more complicated, but she was also on a power trip. *It's not about power. As an angel, it should never be about power.*

I'll see you after you're summoned, I said to Grace. She nodded, her smile never wavering, and I turned towards the cloud field gates. When I reached them I lightly ran my fingers over their smooth, pearly surface, and they opened without a sound.

The cloud dust licked at my legs as I walked. I wound up a spiral staircase and each step dissipated as I went. The terrain changed the closer I got to the Council's chamber. It went from soft and low where it covered only my feet, to dense and thick, reaching almost to my waist. Over my shoulder I could see the path I'd made through the whiteness. The quiet floated around me. No one else was around. I was on the second highest level, reserved for the Council members, and the only way to gain access was to be summoned.

When I reached the Council chamber the door was closed. I placed my palm in the centre and waited to be admitted. The white slab of marble was warm beneath my fingertips. Everything in Heaven felt warm to the touch.

The door slid open and I stepped through into a white, circular room. If I wasn't a divine being the brightness would have blinded me. The door closed behind me then disappeared. I moved to the centre of the room.

My heart was heavy, and a knot formed in my stomach. Normally I would have been excited about a new mission, but this time I didn't plan to return home. I'd guarded my secret for so long; a harder task than I'd thought it would be. So far Michael was the only one who knew, and I was hoping to keep it that way.

"Welcome, Seth," the Council said. Their voice echoed off the walls of the chamber. They spoke as one entity, but they were also many. Twelve empty thrones lined the circular wall. The Council only appeared to the archangels. Lower level angels didn't get the privilege. It was like having a conversation in a cave with your eyes closed.

"What's the mission this time?" I asked, cutting right to the chase. I wasn't in the mood for pleasantries or small talk.

"England—"

"It's always England," I said. My brow knitted and I scowled.

"That's where you're needed most."

I didn't personally have anything against England, but a change of scenery would've been nice—although, after this mission it wouldn't be a problem.

"The land is at war. Many innocents are dying before their time," the Council said.

The cloud dust swirled at my feet and parted to reveal the earth below. I looked through the gap at a castle. People bustled about, archers lined the walls, and knights readied their mounts. The surrounding village was a hive of activity.

"Mankind has always been its own worst enemy," I said. "Some of them deserve everything they get."

"That may be so, but a lot of them don't."

"What needs to be done?" I asked.

The white mist drew back over itself then swirled again and dissipated to reveal another image. A young girl, heavily pregnant, walked through the village that spread out at the castle's base. She looked over her shoulder and I caught a glimpse of her vivid blue eyes.

"This girl is very important," the Council said. "You must find her—"

"And do what? She looks healthy. Is someone going to do something to her?"

"You must make sure she and the baby survive. We can't give you all the answers. You know our interference must be minimal, and you will know what to do when the time comes," the Council replied. "This task is more important than any you've been set before. You haven't failed yet, Seth, and we trust you won't this time."

"Where are we landing?"

"Not far from the castle. Find the river and follow it to the village. A woman at the first cottage will be there to help you."

"Does she have a name?" I asked.

"Seth, by now you should know how this works. You will instantly know your go-between. You'll be able to see it in her eyes."

Yes, I did know how it worked, but there was no harm in asking. Go-betweens were our link between Heaven and Earth during our mission. They weren't angels, but they were blessed with divine knowledge. They acted as a guide and an aid if we needed them.

All was quiet for a few minutes and I watched the girl walk along the road, her hand resting on top of her swollen belly. *Why are you so important?* I thought.

The Council spoke, breaking through my reverie. "As always you may choose one other angel to accompany you. May we suggest Angelica, she tends to use her head a little more than—"

"You already know who I'll choose."

The Council fell silent, and I imagined twelve elderly men sitting on their thrones, one running his fingers through his grey beard. "Very well, we will summon her," they said.

Before the cloud dust closed over I took one last look at the girl, committing to memory her round face, and the way her chestnut hair folded in waves onto her shoulders. I walked to where the door would be.

"Seth," the Council said. "We trust you *will* make the right decision?"

Their question made me hesitate. The silence hung around me and the tension in the air was thick enough to feel with my hand. I'd been foolish to think I could get anything past the Council. They saw everything, and even an angel with the strongest mental guard had no hope of closing them out.

"I will do what I think is right," I finally said.

The marble door appeared. I pressed my palm against it and it slid open. The moment I stepped over the threshold the door was concealed again. The high mound of cloud dust encasing the Council's chamber fell to the floor and left me standing alone in the silence.

I took my time walking back to the cloud field. I could have orbed, or flown, and been there in an instant, but while I was in Heaven I preferred to walk. Something about the action soothed me. There was plenty of time for orbing on Earth. Besides, Grace wouldn't be in the field, she'd be in the chamber going through the same conversation I'd just had.

The Council never gave us many details about our missions. Mostly it was fine, and we knew what to do soon after we got to our destination. But sometimes it took us a little longer to work out what needed to be done. It frustrated me when they wouldn't share everything they knew. I'd long ago suspected they had a crystal ball of sorts. The Council could see what was coming, but they broke no rules by making us figure things out on our own. Basically, the Angels of the Light did the dirty work.

By the time I reached the cloud field gates Grace had returned. She wasn't opposed to orbing in Heaven. I stroked the gate and it opened for me, moving the cloud dust around my feet. Grace walked towards me, her white dress rippled out behind her, and her pearlescent wings fluttered gently. She held my gaze with her brilliant, sapphire eyes.

"England again, huh," she said. "I wonder if there's anywhere else in the world that needs us."

"There are plenty of earth-bound angels, Grace," Angelica said, coming to her side. "I'm sure you only get sent there because you've been before."

"Or maybe we're the best angels for the job," I said.

Angelica raised her eyebrows as if to question me and I scowled at her.

"Knock it off you two," Grace said. "When will you learn to get along?"

Never, I thought. Angelica irritated me. I didn't like or trust her, but she was Grace's friend so I tolerated having her around.

"Come on, Seth." Grace orbed to the far side of the field. *Catch me if you can.*

I chuckled and shook my head, then began walking across the field. Grace was always trying to get me to orb around the place. I never knew why she was in such a hurry. It wasn't like we needed to be anywhere in particular when we were at home. I put it down to the fact she couldn't sit still. Grace got bored easily; she wanted to be constantly busy. Something you couldn't really achieve when you lived in a huge expanse of whiteness.

"Would you hurry up," Grace said, materialising beside me and grabbing my hand. She orbed, forcing me to orb with her. We crossed the field in seconds then exited through the earth-bound gate.

"Why the rush?" I asked. "I'm sure they can wait the few minutes it would've taken us to walk."

"We're going back to Earth; isn't that reason enough to hurry?"

On any normal mission it would have been. We both loved leaving Heaven. Down there we could do so much, see so much, and have experiences we couldn't have surrounded by whiteness and cloud dust. But I didn't want to rush because I probably wouldn't be coming back. It could be the last time I ever saw my home. The last time I ever got to kick the white mist into the air and watch it settle gently back into place.

After passing through the gate, we spiralled down a ramp towards one of the lower levels. It led us to the departure pad—a large round depression in the cloud dust. An angel looked up from the marble departure desk. He brushed his dark hair from his brow and picked up a white clipboard and pen.

"Hey, Daniel," Grace said. "How're things?"

"Pretty much the same. Angels go down to Earth, and then they come up again." He smiled. "So, you two are off to England."

"Yeah. Where, exactly?" Grace asked. "It's kind of a big place."

Daniel pursed his lips. "The form just says England. I'm sure you'll figure it out."

"Great," I mumbled. "You know it wouldn't kill the Council to be specific once in a while."

Daniel laughed. "You're a big boy, Seth. Besides, I know you love a challenge."

Yep, that was true.

Daniel handed Grace the clipboard and asked her to sign next to the red X. I did the same, and we stepped out onto the departure pad.

"Good luck," Daniel said.

"You ready to go?" Grace asked.

I hesitated for a moment, then took her hand and squeezed it gently. "As ready as I'll ever be."

Daniel pushed one of two buttons that sat in the centre of the desk. His smile was the last thing I saw as Grace and I left Heaven.

3

Grace slipped and grabbed my arm. The warmth from her touch spread through me and made my head fuzzy. I gently held her until she regained her feet and kept moving. The moment she let go it was like she took a piece of me with her. Like there was something missing. On Earth everything was so much more alive than it was in Heaven. So many textures, smells and tastes, so much to experience that we couldn't back home. Which is why when Grace touched me, it was like tiny bolts of lightning coursing across my skin.

"I can't believe they dumped us this far away," Grace grumbled. She looked to the castle in the distance. "Why can't we just orb to where we want to be?"

"Because, you know the rules—we have to follow their instructions."

"Yeah, yeah. Since when have you been an advocate

for good behaviour?"

I chuckled. She was right. Every chance I got I looked for ways to try something new, or piss someone off—especially when it came to Michael. He was one of those angels that couldn't help making everyone else's business his own. He'd caught me off guard a while ago, and found out about my decision by pure accident. Archangels were stronger mentally and physically. When Michael discovered I had a thought worth listening in on, there was no stopping him. I resented him for his invasion of privacy. His argument had been it was his job to look after the safety and welfare of all Heaven's angels. Apparently he had a right to know. I didn't care; I was still pissed at him.

Grace and I walked in silence for a while. The countryside was breathtaking, but harsh. Rock piles littered the green hills, and Grace winced with almost every step. She miss-stepped again, and I managed to catch her before she hit the ground.

"Sit," I said, placing her on a large flat rock. "Your feet are cut to pieces. Let them heal a bit before we keep going."

"I'm fine, Seth. I'm a big girl."

"I know, but I want to rest as well."

"He who loves walking so much?" She raised her eyebrows.

"Walking on Earth is different to walking in Heaven."

"Yeah, the cloud dust doesn't cut your feet," Grace scoffed. She lifted her foot, rested it across her knee and inspected the damage. Her skin was already beginning to heal. She shivered against the cold. I wanted to hold her to keep her warm, but it would only make things harder.

I turned my attention to the valley below us. In the

crevice of the hills I saw the river the Council had spoken of. I didn't want to get up. I didn't want us to keep moving, because if we did it meant I'd have less time with Grace. I'd made my decision and my argument with Michael rang through my mind, but I didn't want to think about it too much.

Grace's gaze burned into my cheek and I couldn't help looking at her. Her eyes sparkled and she wore a content smile. After a few moments she frowned. Grace always knew when something was wrong. Her ability to read people was something all angels could do. She just did it better than the rest of us.

I'd spent so long keeping my secret away from her it took all my strength not to open my mind and let her in. She knew I was holding something back, but she was too nice to pry.

"Everything all right?" she asked, slipping her hand into mine.

I dropped my eyes to where our hands sat on my leg, fingers entwined. It was hard for me to know where I finished and she began. I wanted to tell her that no, everything was far from all right. Instead, I pulled her to her feet and we started walking again.

"I can see the river from here," I said. "I hope the first cottage isn't too far away."

"If someone can give me a coat and some shoes, I'll be happy," Grace replied. She freed her hand from mine and wrapped her arms around herself. Even though the sun was shining it was cold.

"I'll second that," I said.

Every time we came to Earth, we faced the same

problem. Heaven sent us with nothing. We didn't get to stock up on the necessities before we left. All I wore were my white linen pants. And Grace's dress, although beautiful, was far from warm. Again I wanted to hold her and never let go.

"What did the Council show you through the cloud dust?" Grace asked.

"A castle. And a young pregnant woman."

"Why do you think she's so important?"

I shrugged. "There could be many reasons. Maybe it's not her, maybe it's the child."

"Did you see anything else?" she asked.

"Grace, I just wanted to get out of there and come back to the cloud field. It was like every other time I've been summoned. I wasn't paying much attention."

Grace sighed. "You should know by now you have to pay close attention."

"I do … when it matters." I took in the profile of her face as we walked and committed the details to memory: her black hair; her smooth, porcelain skin. The corners of her mouth turned up but she kept her eyes straight ahead.

The rest of our walk was mostly silent. It was one of the things I loved about Grace. We didn't need to talk. Usually all it took was a glance or a smile, and we knew what the other was thinking. Often she'd open her mind to me. She wouldn't say anything in particular; she'd just show me places and images, or her feelings. When she did that it was like wrapping my heart in a warm blanket. Grace had an irritating way of making me feel safe; irritating because I was supposed to be tough. I didn't usually do mushy, but she softened me in a way no one else could.

By the time we reached the river the sun was high in the sky. The first cottage wasn't much farther. In the distance the castle loomed over the village like a monster with pointy teeth. Smoke curled from the chimneys. The smell was welcoming and promised warmth.

The gate to the first cottage hung askew on its hinges. I pushed it open and a black dog greeted us. He gave my hand a quick sniff then returned to his post by the front door. I rapped my knuckles against the splintery wood and waited. After a few moments there was no answer, so I went to knock again. Grace gently grabbed my wrist to stop me. She pointed down to the river where a woman walked towards us. She wore a full brown skirt and a cream lace bonnet, and carried a wicker basket under her arm.

When the woman reached the gate she stopped to catch her breath, offering us a welcoming smile.

"I was wondering when you'd turn up," she said.

The woman stumbled and I raced to catch the basket before it could fall to the ground and scatter vegetables everywhere. Grace opened the door and we all shuffled through into the dim cottage. I set the basket on a rustic wooden table and the woman bustled around the place, putting the produce away and generally tidying up. She stoked the fire then settled back into a chair lined with soft cushions.

We've found the right person, then? Grace asked.

I looked into the woman's eyes and saw nothing but a kind heart and grateful soul. *You know we have,* I replied, taking a seat at the table.

I know. I was just testing you.

"Go through to the bedroom, dear. Some clothes and boots are on the chest for you," the woman said to Grace. "We can't have him half-naked."

Grace blushed. She went into the next room and returned with the clothing in her arms. She sat at the table and laced the brown leather boots up to her shins. She quickly put a jacket on and buttoned it over her dress. It had a wide collar and open elbow length sleeves. It wasn't the highest of fashion for the time, but she would have looked beautiful in a potato sack. She passed me some boots, a pair of brown slacks—which I pulled on over my linen pants—and a long sleeved shirt.

"Thank you." I took my seat at the table again. The woman inclined her head and smiled warmly. "Can you tell us your name?" I asked.

"I am Ellis Stanway," she said. She unfastened the bonnet from under her chin and laid it on the arm of the chair. Her silver hair fell to her shoulders and she smiled again. Creases formed around her friendly, hazel eyes.

"Do you have any information for us?" Grace asked. She went to the small window at the front of the cottage and stared out into the road. "Where are we supposed to find her," she murmured.

"Questions later," Ellis said. "First, we eat."

"That's very kind of you," I said.

"Always happy to help the likes of your people."

Ellis rose from her chair and went to the kitchen. She busied herself and quickly prepared a meal of bread and cheese, which she served to us on wooden plates.

"It's just you living here?" Grace asked.

"Yes, yes. Just me," Ellis said, taking a mouthful of

bread. "The Keep boys over yonder make sure I'm all right, and they watch out for the sheep that roam this side of the river."

When we finished our meal, Ellis disappeared into the bedroom and came back with a blanket for each of us.

"It gets so cold in here even with the morning sun," she said.

She draped one over Grace's shoulders and handed me the other. Inside the cottage was like a small cave with its stone walls and dirt floor. The only natural light came from two small windows. The rest was generated by the crackling fire and a couple of oil lamps. Ellis took one of the lamps from a shelf near the door and set it on the table.

"Now, we get down to business," Ellis said.

She placed a pot of water on the stove. It slowly came to the boil and bubbled noisily. The fire crackled and Grace went to stand in front of it to warm her hands. In the centre of the table Ellis put a large, round dish. It was almost flat like a platter, but had enough depth to the sides to hold fruit or vegetables without them rolling off. Ellis set a slab of wood on the table next to the bowl and brought the pot over from the stove.

"I trust by now you know what I am?" Ellis asked.

"Of course." Grace turned away from the fire. "You're our go-between. We have one on every mission."

"Good. Now, come sit down and see what I have to show you."

Ellis waved Grace over and we sat together on one side of the table. Grace pulled her blanket tighter around her shoulders and leant in. Ellis poured the boiling water into the shallow dish. Steam curled into the air and the surface of the water clouded over. She dipped her finger in the centre and began to run it through the water in a figure-of-eight. Grace sucked in a breath at the shock of Ellis putting her hand in boiling water. We'd never seen our path using this method before. Each time was different, and dictated by our go-between. Ellis had probably been doing this for many years.

When Ellis withdrew her hand the tiny clouds floating on top of the water began to part and an image appeared in the dish. The face of a young woman rippled on the surface of the water. She was the same woman the Council had shown me through the cloud dust, and her eyes were just as striking as they'd been the first time I'd seen them. She wore a servant's dress and was quite obviously pregnant. Grace frowned and pursed her lips.

"Is this the woman you saw as well?" I asked.

Grace nodded, and then her hand flew to her mouth. I returned my attention to the image in the water. The woman wore a pained expression and she clutched her swollen belly.

"It's the baby, isn't it?" Grace looked at Ellis with questioning eyes.

"You must find her, and make sure both she and this child survive," Ellis said.

"Can we ask what will happen if we fail?"

"You can, dear, but I won't answer you." Ellis' eyes sparkled and she chuckled deeply. "I'm not permitted to tell you anything other than where to find her."

"Then tell us where she is. We'll go straight away. We can get there in seconds," Grace said.

But Ellis was shaking her head. "I'm not sure it's wise to be so hasty. There's a lot of unrest at the moment. It might do to wait a bit."

"We can look after ourselves," I said. "And tomorrow may be too late." I stared at Ellis. If she'd been any normal person without a divine blessing, I'd have been able to see and hear everything she was thinking, but her thoughts were off-limits to us. The Council always made sure we only knew what was necessary to get the job done.

Grace glanced at me sideways. She was eager to get going, but she knew the rules as well as I did. The first person we met was the one to trust. There was always a reason we landed where we did.

Ellis regarded us for a moment. Even though she had the power to sway our decisions, she wouldn't stand in our way. She would agree with whatever we chose to do.

"Very well then," she said. "But be careful. If anyone questions who you are, tell them you're visiting me."

Ellis picked up the shallow bowl and the image of the girl disappeared. She tipped the water out and busied herself with cleaning up. Grace and I sat patiently at the table.

Ellis sighed. "She's a scullion in the castle kitchen and her name is Amity, but I can't tell you any more than that. Now go on, get, before I make you stay." She waved us out the door.

I handed Ellis our blankets and held the gate open for Grace. A chicken clucked and flew down from its perch on the fence.

"You know where to come if you need help," Ellis called after us.

"Thanks." I waved as we walked down the road.

Farmers tended sheep in the surrounding fields. The village was a hive of activity, but the faces of the people were strained. Peasants worked in their own gardens, and many of them stopped what they were doing to stare as we walked by. Some children played close to their homes but their enthusiasm was low, others peered out windows with worried expressions. There was noise and chatter everywhere except between Grace and I. I wanted to talk to Grace, to say something to fill our silence, but I didn't know what to say. Until that moment it had always been so easy with her; we'd always been connected, but my decision weighed heavily in my mind, and for the first time ever I was growing uncomfortable in her presence.

"Seth..." Grace paused. "You've hardly said anything since we left home. I'm worried. I know there's something you're not telling me."

"Of course you do," I sighed.

"What's that supposed to mean?" Grace frowned and folded her arms.

I shook my head. "Just that I can't get anything past you." I could feel her gently probing the wall in my mind, but I didn't let it budge. It was better she didn't know about what I was going to do. She'd never condone it, and when she realised she couldn't stop me, she'd probably want to come with me. I couldn't ask her to do that. "Really, I'm fine." I smiled half-heartedly.

"If you say so," she said.

Grace looked up at me and smiled. Light glinted in her sapphire eyes, making them sparkle, and it was like staring at a star filled galaxy. If I could I would've frozen her in that moment. Since I'd known her there had probably been a million moments I'd have said the same thing. But the way she exuded beauty, divinity and grace captivated me. She didn't know I was in love with her. She loved me, just not the way I wanted. Grace loved everyone unconditionally. But true, passionate love was forbidden for any angel. So many times I'd come close to telling her, but it was better this way. If she knew how I felt, it would change everything between us. I couldn't risk it. And if the Council ever found out I'd confessed my love for her, they'd condemn both of us.

I had to give her up, and the only way to do that was to leave.

I returned her smile, and struggled to hold back the tears that stung my eyes.

4

Grace and I walked the length of the road that snaked through the village and discussed our options on ways to find Amity. Grace wanted to orb right in there, but I pointed out the flaws in her hasty plan.

"We can't just materialise in a ball of light," I said. "Don't you think it might scare a few people?"

Grace scowled. "Well, what's your suggestion?"

"She's a scullion. We'll get into the castle first then go straight to the kitchen."

We stopped at the bridge and I casually tossed some pebbles into the moat while eyeing the entrance to the castle. The portcullis was closed and the porter was quite noticeably asleep. His head lolled to the side. He startled himself awake only to nod off again almost instantly. The watchman came past on what I assumed was one of his rounds. He stopped and kicked the porter who swore and jumped to his feet. They exchanged some heated words. The watchman looked out through the portcullis then continued on his rounds. I chuckled when the porter made a rude gesture at the watchman's back before he sat down and nodded off again.

Soldiers lined the wall-walk and conversed amongst themselves while they kept an eye on the surrounding country side. There didn't seem to be any evidence of an imminent attack, but everyone was on guard none the less—except for the porter.

I took another glance around. The village bustled with activity, but people mostly stayed close to their homes. Inside the castle everyone should have be sitting down to dinner, and that meant Amity would hopefully be where we expected—in the kitchen. The porter was still dozing, and the watchman was out of sight.

"I wonder if we could walk up and knock," Grace said. "Do you think he'd let us in?"

"I think we'd be pushing our luck," I replied. "Do we really want to draw unnecessary attention to ourselves? All we have to do is get past the barbican. Once we're inside it should be easy to blend in. If the porter stays asleep he won't give us any trouble."

"If you say so," Grace said. "Ready?"

I nodded, took one last look around to make sure no one was watching, and orbed. Balls of pure, white light emanated from our centres and grew out until they engulfed us. Moments later our light spun on the other side of the portcullis. When we had re-formed, Grace and I quickly dropped back into the shadows. The porter mumbled something in his sleep, but didn't wake.

The area on the other side of the barbican was quiet, but we had to get out before the watchman came past on another round. I grabbed Grace's hand and quickly walked across to the inner bailey. When we reached the wall I stopped and took a moment to decide which way to go next.

I heard footsteps coming towards us and panicked. I wasn't sure if we were permitted to be in that part of the castle, so I tugged gently on Grace's hand, spun her around and pressed her against the wall. Her chest rose and fell in beat with mine. She clutched my upper arms and stared into my eyes. My hands rested against the wall on either side of her head, our faces mere millimetres from each other, and in a moment of pure misjudgement I leant in intending to kiss her. Grace's grip on my arms tightened and her breathing sped up.

"What have we here," a gruff voice said.

I closed my eyes and rested my forehead against Grace's.

"Just taking a moment," I said. "I'm sure you understand." I turned my head a little and tried to smile wickedly.

The watchman sniggered. "I think you'd better move along. The feast is about to start, and if you're meant to be working you'll be in trouble."

"Of course," I said. I put my arm around Grace's shoulders and led her away.

We followed the wall until we turned the corner and I let go of Grace. I couldn't look at her, and I couldn't believe what I'd almost done. If the watchman hadn't have come along when he did, I'd be attempting to explain something I didn't want to. As it was, Grace wasn't going to let me off so easily.

"What happened back there?" she whispered.

"Nothing," I said a little too quickly. "I was trying to keep us out of trouble."

"By pressing me against the wall and almost kissing me?"

"What are you talking about?" I asked.

Grace blushed and looked away. "Never mind," she mumbled.

Guilt punched me in the stomach as we snaked our way through the castle grounds. I didn't want Grace to feel uncomfortable, but I couldn't let her think my actions were anything other than for her protection.

We walked in silence until we passed the blacksmith's shed, and the stables. Grace stopped to stroke the nose of a fine-looking mare. A squire brushed the horse's coat, and he offered Grace a bashful smile. The mare whinnied and tossed her head, but lowered it again for another pat.

"I can look after myself, you know," Grace said. She stared at the mare as she scratched between its ears.

I sighed. "I know. I just acted on the spur of the moment. I thought it would be a good cover. And we're a team, remember? I watch out for you; hopefully you'll watch out for me."

"I've always watched out for you." Grace lowered her hand and faced me. "You're my best friend."

The corners of my mouth curled up. "Come on," I said. "I'm guessing the kitchen is near the great hall."

"And where most of the smoke is coming from?" Grace looked to the blue sky; a trail of smoke tumbled across it and mingled with the clouds.

I grunted and kept walking. The kitchen was built a little way away from the great hall, the two buildings joined by a timber passage. Livestock was tethered to posts along the outer wall. The entrance was littered with rubbish and muck. A young man shovelled it into a trough; the stink was disgusting. A large round woman with a dirty apron threw a bucket of scraps out the door. They landed on my feet and I scowled at her.

"What are you looking at?" she said.

Already, I didn't like her. "We're looking for Amity," I replied, trying not to growl.

"Well, she's working. Only workers are allowed inside my kitchen."

"We'll work," I said.

The woman looked me up and down. "I'll feed you, but there's no pay."

"That's fine."

Grace stared at me with wide eyes. *You want us to work, in there?* She turned her nose up.

Come on, princess. What better way to find out how to help Amity?

Before Grace could protest further, I followed the woman into the kitchen. The room was huge with a high cavernous ceiling. People bustled everywhere. Fires burned in the large ovens. Cooks stirred food boiling in big cauldrons. Kitchen hands lined a table and chopped vegetables in time with one another. Dried herbs hung from wooden racks on the wall. There was so much happening I didn't know where to look first.

Grace took two aprons down from a hook and handed

one to me. Before I'd even had time to tie it around my waist, several servants entered the kitchen from the tunnel. We were swept up in their procession and didn't stop until we reached the far end of the room. Bowls, plates, cups and spoons were strewn onto the floor. Large tubs were pulled from a recess in the wall, and a small boy filled the first with a bucket of water. No sooner had he left than another boy tipped his bucket in. The children kept coming until the tubs were full.

The servants knelt at the tubs and began to scrub the utensils. They seemed to have it down to an art. Some would wash, others rinse, others dry, and finally someone would stack everything on a nearby table. Grace was grinning from ear to ear watching the mechanics of their team work. So far, no one had noticed we weren't helping. Grace raised her eyebrows at me then grabbed my arm and pulled me to my knees. She thrust a dirty bowl into my hands and dunked one into the tub herself. It looked like we were going to wash dishes.

A minute ago you were turning your nose up, I said in her head.

We should probably try to blend in, she replied. *And it gives us a chance to find Amity without drawing attention to ourselves.*

There was a mix of young and old, male and female, all working hard. I tried to look at the faces around the tubs, but everyone had their heads down concentrating on their work.

I turned my attention to the rest of the kitchen, taking in all the movement and noise. Then I saw Amity walking towards us. She held a basket in her hands, and was noticeably uncomfortable due to her pregnant state. When she reached the table where the clean bowls and plates were stacked, she cried out and bent forward. The basket slipped from her hands and she knocked a stack of bowls to the floor. They scattered in every direction, and the sound echoed through the kitchen.

The woman who'd greeted us at the door hurried over and grabbed Amity by the hair. She pulled her to her feet and Amity screamed in pain. I didn't know if it was from having her hair pulled, or from the way she clutched her belly. Grace's eyes widened in shock, and my initial reaction was to run to Amity's defence. It was enough to make my blood boil beneath my skin. I went to stand, but Grace grabbed my arm.

The woman yelled at Amity and I cringed.

"What are you doing," she screamed. "Look at this mess."

Amity whimpered and stared at the woman with scared eyes. A tear rolled silently down her cheek. She squeezed her eyes shut, leant forward and cried out.

"She's in labour," Grace said.

"So, now we intervene?" I asked.

Grace scowled, jumped to her feet and raced to Amity's side. She put an arm around her shoulders to stop her from tumbling to the floor. Then she turned on the woman. "How dare you treat her like this you evil witch!"

"Don't you speak to me like that," the woman said. "I'm the boss around here."

Grace fixed the woman with a dark stare, and it made her take a step back. I smiled to myself. Even when she was angry, Grace was beautiful.

"With God as your witness you will not lay another

hand on this girl!" Grace said. "Now, let us pass." She glowed softly with her divine light.

The woman's eyes widened. She bowed her head and mumbled an apology. The entire kitchen had come to a standstill. All eyes were on Grace, and the workers' faces were filled with awe. The woman stepped aside and Grace helped Amity to the door. I stood to follow. The woman frowned but didn't attempt to stop me. After I'd stepped outside, she clapped her hands and ordered everyone back to work.

"We have to get her somewhere to have this baby," I said. The man with the shovel stopped and stared before returning to his task.

"Amity, where do you live?" Grace asked.

Amity cried out again and doubled over. "Who are you?" she asked through clenched teeth.

"We're here to help." I glanced at Grace over the top of Amity's head.

Amity looked at me, her eyes glistened with fear. But it wasn't a fear of what was happening to her. I could read it in her soul. She was afraid because she had no one. No husband, no family. She was alone. Amity moaned and squeezed her eyes shut, her face contorting into a grimace.

"Do you have anyone we can send for? The father?" I asked, but I already knew what her answer would be.

Amity shook her head. "Lost in the war." She stopped, dropped to her knees and clutched her belly. "Please! Do something," she cried.

Come on, Seth. We have to orb her to a safe place. Grace spoke in my mind. *She can't have her baby here in the pig muck.*

We'd only made it as far as the tethered animals.

We can't disappear in a ball of light either, I replied. *There are people watching.*

Then we'll go somewhere else.

Grace placed a hand on Amity's shoulder. "Where do you normally sleep? Do you have your own space?"

Amity groaned again and shook her head. "I sleep on the kitchen floor."

"Well, that's not much help," Grace mumbled.

I helped Amity to her feet and we guided her away from the animals in search of a cleaner, more private place. The nasty woman from the kitchen came running after us. I hoped her conscience had gotten the better of her and she wouldn't yell again.

"Get her to the midwife," she said. "She'll be taken care of there."

"Can you tell us which way?" Grace asked.

"You're not from here, are you?" The woman looked scared, as if Grace would strike her down at any moment. "No, of course you're not."

The woman grabbed a young boy as he ran past. She ordered him to guide us to a small, stone room where we'd find a woman named Constance. She assured us it wasn't very far, so we hurried off. Amity managed to walk most of the way. We had to stop a few times for her contractions, but we eventually made it. Those who weren't feasting in the great hall, or working, stopped to watch as we passed, but no one offered to help or gave us any trouble.

We reached the doorway to the room the woman had told us about and I helped Amity inside. It was dark and musty; the only light came from candles burning in small holes in the walls. There was a straw mat in one corner with a tub of water and a stool next to it. There was also a U-shaped chair that I could only assume was used for giving birth. I looked at Grace sideways.

"Hello," Grace called.

Amity moaned in my arms. I could feel her weakening, and if I wasn't holding her up she'd have fallen to the floor in a heap.

A woman came into the room through a doorway I hadn't seen in the dim light. She went to the tub, washed her hands and wiped them on her apron before sitting down on the stool.

"Well, come on, bring her over," she said.

Grace and I helped Amity to the mat and laid her down on her side. She was sweating and had her eyes shut tightly, as if not looking would take the pain away.

"Thank you," Grace said. "Constance, is it?"

"Yes, yes. Now, she'll be fine. It's been a while since I've lost anyone. I'll take good care of her." Constance looked at me. "You can't stay. No men while women are having babies."

Grace hid a smirk behind her hand.

It's not funny, I said to Grace. *How am I supposed to help if I'm not in the room?*

It is funny, and it's just the way they do things.

"I'll keep you informed," Grace said so Constance could hear. "Just wait outside."

5

Sweat beaded on my forehead and I wiped it away with the back of my hand. I'd been sitting outside the birthing room long enough for the sun to dip below the castle wall, and there was still no baby. Grace had come out to update me on Amity's progress twice. I wished she'd come out again to let me know what was going on. A few times I'd tried to speak to her in her head, but she kept telling me to be patient. Patience wasn't my best virtue.

"Hey," Grace said.

I glanced up to see her standing in the doorway. "Update?" I asked.

She sat beside me and leant against the stone wall. "Any minute now. But I think there's something wrong."

"Why else would we be here?"

Grace pursed her lips. "We can't interfere unless we absolutely have to."

"If we can't take her pain away and actually help, what good are we?" I growled in frustration.

"Aren't you the one usually telling me to follow the rules?" Grace drew her knees to her chest and laid her cheek on them. She smiled sweetly. "We were told to make sure they survive, nothing more."

"Well, to do that, shouldn't we be in there with Amity? Not out here discussing it?"

Footsteps sounded from inside the birthing room and Constance poked her head out. "Come. It's time," she said.

"I want Seth to come, too," Grace said as she got to her feet.

Constance stared at Grace, her face serious. From the look in her eyes something was terribly wrong.

"I noticed the difference in you from the moment you arrived. I can't explain it, but I feel calm in your presence. If you want this man in the birthing room, then I think there may be a good reason," she said.

"You can trust us," Grace said. "Seth would never harm Amity. He wants to help. We both do."

Constance turned to me. "Well, I hope you can help. I don't think she'll make it. But no one is to ever know you were in here while she was giving birth. It's unheard of, and I could lose my place in the community." She looked both ways out the door before ushering us inside.

Amity lay on her side on the straw mat. She moaned softly and had her eyes tightly shut. Constance knelt beside her and gently coaxed her to a sitting position. Amity cried out as another contraction ripped through her body.

"Come on dear, it won't be too much longer. You need to start pushing," Constance said.

"I can't," Amity moaned.

Constance motioned to Grace. "Help me get her onto the birthing chair."

Grace went to Amity's side and took her hand. They helped her onto the chair and Grace knelt beside her. I positioned myself behind Amity and took her other hand.

"What's he doing in here?" Amity asked.

"Shush now, he's here to help," Constance said.

"You can do this," Grace said. "We're right here. You're not alone."

I wiped sweat from Amity's brow with a cloth then looked at Constance. Her mouth pressed into a thin line, and she shook her head. I could read in her mind what the problem was.

"The baby is breech." Constance sat on the stool and reached a hand under the birthing chair. "When you feel a contraction I want you to push."

Amity moaned again and tears squeezed from the corners of her eyes. I channelled my strength into her through my hands. We may not have been able to interfere until absolutely necessary, but I couldn't sit back and do nothing. My energy would calm her.

Be ready, I said in Grace's head.

She nodded, and the power of her energy flowed into Amity as well.

Constance guided Amity through the pushes. Amity screamed each time, slumping back against the chair to rest between contractions. I could feel her life force draining; it came and went in waves, and each time it ebbed my heart ached for her.

"The legs are out," Constance cried. "Just a little longer."

A few minutes later Amity brought a baby into the world. "It's a boy," Grace whispered.

I squeezed Amity's hand, but there was no response. Her head lolled on her shoulders and she slipped sideways. I caught her before she could tumble off the chair.

"He's not breathing." Constance laid the boy on the mat and swaddled him in some cloth.

"Seth, help Amity," Grace said. She swept the baby into her arms. For a moment all I could do was watch in awe as she did what we were sent to do. Grace gazed at the baby. His face was peaceful and he was still. Grace smiled her beautiful, angelic smile, and her skin glowed. She cradled the boy's head with one hand, and her golden glow spread into him. Within moments he opened his eyes. Then he opened his mouth and cried.

I turned my attention to Amity and lifted her from the chair to lay her on the straw. I could feel Grace's eyes on me, watching my every move.

A little help would be nice, I said to her.

Grace handed the baby to Constance—who seemed in shock at the miracle Grace had performed—and joined me at Amity's side. The young woman lay still. No breath, no movement, but a faint heartbeat. We placed our hands on her and our light flowed into her body. Constance sucked in a sharp breath and held the baby closer to her breast. Amity's skin shone with our light. It coursed through her and healed her. We nourished her tired body with our divinity, and before long she was breathing again.

"How did you..." Constance stared at us with wide eyes.

Grace raised her head and smiled. A halo of divine light bathed her in its glow. Constance fell to her knees and sobbed, clutching the newborn to her chest. She crawled to us and touched our feet.

"Please, stand up, Constance." Grace leant down, took her by the elbow and guided her to her feet. "You don't need to kneel in our presence."

Amity's eyes fluttered open and she tried to move.

"Easy does it, you're still weak," Grace said. She helped Amity sit up.

"Where's my baby?" Amity asked.

Constance came closer to hand the boy over when Amity lurched forward and cried out in more pain. I caught her before she fell on her side.

Constance thrust the baby into Grace's arms and knelt at Amity's feet. She felt beneath Amity's dress and her eyes widened in alarm.

"There's another baby," she said.

"No! I can't do it again," Amity cried.

I held Amity's weight. She fell into me and her eyes rolled back in her head. Grace hastily rinsed a cloth in the tub and handed it to me. I wiped Amity's face and gently patted her cheek until she opened her eyes.

"You can do this," I said.

She nodded, and then grimaced as she pushed with another contraction. Within minutes there was another set of tiny fingers and toes being swaddled in cloth.

"A girl," Constance said with a smile. "Now you have your pigeon pair."

This time the baby seemed fine. I helped Amity lie down and Grace brought one bundle, then the other, to Amity's side. The boy cried until Amity put him to her breast, but the little girl was content to lie on the straw and gurgle softly. Her eyes were divine and wiser than her few short minutes of life. She would grow up to do great things.

"What will you name them?" Grace asked.

Amity stared lovingly at her new children. "William, I think, after his father, and Fortune, because I am so fortunate to have your blessings."

Constance bustled around and cleaned up. She spread fresh straw over the floor, changed the water in the bucket, and took the rags into the back room.

"Amity, will you and the children be all right?" Grace asked.

"Of course they will," Constance said. "Women give birth every day."

"Will you watch over them for us?" I asked.

"I'll make sure they have a suitable place to stay."

After what Constance had witnessed Grace and I do, I didn't doubt she would make it her life's mission to see Amity and the twins safe. As a midwife she had a great standing within the community. She would do everything in her power to look out for them as if they were her own.

"It's time for us to go," Grace said.

Constance took my hand and bowed. She did the same to Grace then blessed herself with the sign of the cross. "Thank you for bringing your light to save these children."

Grace went to the babies and placed a hand on each of their heads. "May you live a long and healthy life, and fulfil the destiny that has been chosen for you." She blessed Amity as well before returning to my side.

When we stepped from the stone room the sky was dark and alive with stars. Through all the commotion of the day I hadn't had much time to think about my decision. The realisation it was so near gripped my heart like an iron fist and cracked it beyond repair. But again there was no time to think about it. The castle was a flurry of activity. People ran everywhere; horses were being led from the stables, and knights readied themselves to defend the castle. Something must have been happening outside the castle walls, but we weren't staying around to find out what.

"I don't understand why we can't interfere with the bigger problem," Grace said. "All this fighting is a useless waste of life."

"In the long run, it's the small things that matter," I replied.

Grace slipped her hand into mine. "I suppose you're right," she said.

6

Grace tugged my hand and we raced along the stone wall. She giggled and it made me smile. It sounded like bells chiming. I followed close behind. Her hair flicked out behind her and caressed the nape of her neck. I imprinted in my memory every line and every curve of her body, because I didn't know when I'd see her next, or if I'd ever see her again.

She glanced over her shoulder and her eyes sparkled. Her face was radiant; her porcelain skin glowed under the moonlight. She was beautiful, and heavenly, and I loved her so much it hurt.

Grace pulled me into a stone alcove. Her touch spread warmth and happiness through me, and made me feel like I was home. But the happiness was to be short-lived.

"We have to go back now," she whispered.

She was right. Our time had finally run out, but I

43

didn't want it to end.

"Just a few more minutes," I said. "I'm sure they won't mind."

"They see everything. We should be back already."

Grace was right, she was always right. We stood for a moment and gazed into each other's eyes, and I wanted her more than I'd ever wanted anything, so much so it carved a painful wound through my chest all the way to my heart.

"Fly with me first?" I asked.

Grace hesitated, then smiled and nodded. We removed our borrowed clothing and placed it in a neat pile. Hopefully it would be found by someone who needed it. I slipped my hands around Grace's waist and she rested her head on my chest. I closed my eyes and orbed; the tiny glowing spheres swirled around us until they joined together and took us away from Earth.

We materialised in the outer realm where we could fly freely without the risk of being seen. Flying was the most amazing feeling, and we flew side by side, twisting and turning in unison. For a while I forgot all my troubles. I forgot about the consequences of my decision and that I may never see Grace again. I forgot about my breaking heart. A gentle breeze from the flutter of Grace's wings caressed my arm and sent a shiver through me. She shimmered in the night sky, and it took all my strength not to reach out and touch her. I longed to feel the silky smoothness of her feathers beneath my fingertips, to hold her close. I would not be with her when she returned home and it broke my heart all over again.

For a while longer we danced and twirled across the

night sky. Grace's giggle drifted amongst the stars, and they twinkled brighter as she neared. I wished we could stay like that for eternity, but the time had come to say goodbye. I had to let her go. We should have been back already, so I reached for her and took her in my arms for the last time. I savoured her touch and drew in the fresh scent of her hair. It smelt like summer rain. I spent one last moment committing to memory how her body fitted perfectly with mine. But the worst thing I could do at that moment was let myself feel, so I hardened my heart instead.

Grace lifted her head and looked deep into my eyes. She pulled away a little, about to ask what was wrong. I struggled to keep my emotions in check, to hold it all in. The feeling was so overwhelming I lost the battle and a tear slipped down my cheek. Grace reached up and caught it in the palm of her hand where it sat glistening before it solidified into a diamond.

Before Grace had the chance to speak, to ask questions I didn't want to answer, I said the words I'd been waiting a long time to say.

"I renounce you and all your ways."

Grace shook her head. Her expression would haunt me forever. I hated that I was the reason why she looked that way. At first she grabbed for me, but I slipped through her fingers and she became nothing more than a blur at the end of a long, dark tunnel. I could see her lips moving as she screamed my name, but I couldn't hear her. Before long I was covered in a blanket of cold, heavy darkness.

I didn't know what was in store for me. I'd never met a fallen angel. I was never on Earth long enough to find one. If I had, I'd have asked what the fall was like. Maybe then I would have decided differently.

The actual fall wasn't bad, just cold and dark. It was what greeted me on the other side that scared the life out of me. Yes, me—the big tough guy—was scared.

I tumbled over myself for a while until the air started to get warm. One moment I was falling fast enough to make my hair stand on end, the next I'd stopped. No sudden impact, no bone crunching crash. I was suspended in time and surrounded by more darkness.

Before I could think about how weird it was to be stuck in the air, the ground came up to meet my face. My hands slid across rock and I grunted as I sprawled onto my belly.

For a moment I lay there in the dirt. I was tired, and lying on the ground seemed like a good idea. Light seeped into my surroundings and it grabbed my attention.

"No rest for the wicked," I grumbled, as I got to my feet.

My linen pants had turned black. They were tattered around the edges and ripped at the knees. My skin was clammy and sweat beaded on my brow. I wiped it away with the back of my hand.

Slowly, I edged my way towards the light. My hand touched rock and I trailed my fingers along it as I went. Even if I had met a fallen angel, no amount of explaining would have prepared me for what I saw when I emerged from the mouth of the cave.

A huge wall of fire filled a wide chasm in the rock and rose into the air as far as I could see. The roar was deafening. Through the flames was a black gate flanked by two gnarled and twisted Moreton Bay figs. They were leafless and grotesque, their shape changing behind the wall of flickering fire.

Faces moved in and out of the flames. Several would take shape before disintegrating so others could take their place. I heard screams rise above the crackle and roar of the fire, and they chilled me to my bone. I did *not* want to enter the gates of Hell.

Someone began to laugh, and a face made of fire emerged fully from the flames. This time it didn't recede.

"The way I see it, you have two choices," it said. "Wander around aimlessly as an outcast and never have a place, or join me." The face grinned and its teeth dripped fire. The gates squealed, metal on metal, and began to open. "On second thought, I'll make it easy for you."

The fire leapt towards me and I was engulfed by scorching flames. They licked at my skin. It blistered and turned black, but healed just as quickly as it burned. The heat was so intense I thought I was about to die, or be thrust into the fiery chasm. In a moment of clarity I realised I didn't care. I'd already given up the one thing I'd lived for. I thought about Grace. About how much I loved her. I hoped she was all right, and that my leaving hadn't damaged her too much. I prayed she was safe, and I prayed harder than I'd ever prayed before that one day I'd see her again—prayers that would probably go unanswered.

I was so busy concentrating on the image of Grace in my mind I hardly noticed when the fire left me. It pulled back into the chasm in an almighty roar. The gates slammed shut with a metallic screech.

"Have it your way," the voice boomed. "But don't be

fooled into thinking love will always save you. In the end, it will destroy you."

The wall of flames dropped to the height of the gate. The faces still twisted and writhed within it, but they were less eager, as if they had no reason to fight anymore. After they quieted down, and the fire wasn't as aggressive, I could hear the voices of the damned: sad, sorry laments of past lives and regrets.

I pitied them; I didn't want to be one of them.

Despite the heat, a chill seeped into my bones. I turned away from the fire and pulled my wings around myself. My wing-tips crossed in front of me. The sight of them made me stumble and fall to my knees. The hard rock cut into my skin through the holes in my pants. I flexed my wing muscles and a shiver ran through my feathers. I flapped them a few times to make sure they were mine. My wings should have been pearl-white. They were now black. What had I done?

An overwhelming urge to weep engulfed me, but I would not cry. I'd already shed one tear, and that was enough. Instead, I piled up all my anger, and hate, and let out a roar so powerful it shook me and rocked me on my knees. I got to my feet and took one last look at the gates of Hell. I vowed then and there never to set foot through them. Maybe I deserved to after what I'd done, but there were far worse ways to punish myself.

In no way did I believe I deserved to escape from my decision. What I needed was to face it. I'd betrayed the only people who'd loved me; left my family and friends for selfish reasons. I'd hit absolute rock bottom, and I hated myself. I hated Michael for not stopping me, but then I hated myself all over again because Heaven had denied me the right to love freely. A layer of stone grew over my heart and encased it in bitterness. Never again would I allow myself to love. It wasn't worth the pain.

I looked at the ring on my right hand, the ring my Father had given me so long ago. The stone that was once a brilliant tiger's eye had turned black. A roar rose inside me, and this time when I let it free I orbed at the same time. Only I didn't. The feeling was pretty much the same. My body split into a million tiny pieces and re-formed at the other end, but there was no light. Instead of creating spinning orbs of pure, white light, I turned into a thick, black mist.

When I landed I was still yelling. I threw my weight forward and punched the first thing I set eyes on. It happened to be a tree, and the force of my fist split the trunk. A crack resounded off the trees around me and I stopped to take in my surroundings. Where had I landed? In the middle of a forest it seemed. My heart was racing and I had to steady myself against another tree to catch my breath. It was the first time I'd let my anger completely consume me. But I wasn't who I used to be. I'd never be the same again.

"Do I need to say, I told you so?"

When I raised my head I stared straight at Michael. He stood with his arms folded and looked as cocky as ever. Suddenly, there was something else I wanted to punch.

"What do you want?" I asked.

Michael sighed. His brow furrowed and he pursed his lips. It was a long while before he spoke. "Believe it or not, I wanted to see if you were all right."

I laughed. "As if you'd care," I said, and then turned to walk away.

Orbs of light spun in front of me and Michael appeared, blocking my path. I shoved him in the chest and he shoved me harder. The force sent me reeling backwards a few steps and I lunged at him again. This time I held nothing back. My fist connected with his face. Michael's head snapped to the side and blood sprayed from his nose. He didn't return the blow.

"I care, Seth. I care more than you think," Michael said. He wiped his nose with the back of his hand.

"Come on," I screamed at him. "Hit me!" I threw another punch and this time Michael caught my hand with his.

"Don't blame me for your decision," he said.

I shook free of him and scowled. "You should have stopped me."

"You should have chosen differently. Running away doesn't solve anything. And we both know I would never have been able to. You're too stubborn."

Before I could stop myself, I lashed out again. This time Michael wasn't as nice. His fist smacked me in the mouth and blood welled on my tongue. I grabbed him by the arms and threw him to the ground, but Michael was stronger than me and he held on. We tumbled over each other until we stopped with Michael on top of me. He hit me until all I could see was a haze of red.

"Come on, Seth," Michael yelled. "Don't give up now." He lifted me off the ground then slammed me back down. "Isn't this what you wanted? Because it's what you get when you renounce your God."

I started to laugh. It rippled up my body to my shoulders

and made them shake. "I thought you said you cared," I managed to say.

Michael stopped and got to his feet. He held out a hand to help me up, but I hesitated before accepting it. He grabbed me so his palm clutched my inner left forearm. Heat radiated from his hand and I tried to pull away, but he held me firm.

"I did say I care, I just show it differently." He started to laugh with me then stopped himself. His face grew serious and his look made me stop, too.

"What are you doing?" I asked. My arm grew hotter, almost to the point of being unbearable.

"Giving you a reminder of what you've done."

Light seeped under the edges of Michael's hand, and my arm shook with enough force to rock me on my feet. It was like someone dragging a red hot piece of metal across my skin. I gritted my teeth and refused to cry out, but the pain was so intense it made my eyes water. I was at the point where I thought I might pass out when Michael loosened his grip. The light subsided, and when he removed his hand an intricate Celtic cross scarred my skin.

"When the burnt skin falls away it will be black. A permanent reminder of your never ending existence and torment. Whether you like it or not, you're still connected to Heaven, and this will forever remind you of what you had, and what you've left behind."

"I know what I've left behind." I clenched my fist and it sent a sharp pain shooting up my arm.

"While you've been down here feeling sorry for yourself and regretting what you've done, Grace has been up there pining over you.”

“Is she all right?” I whispered.

Michael shook his head. “You ripped her heart to shreds and scattered the pieces across the universe. So no, she’s not.”

I rubbed my face and wiped the blood from my eyes. Apart from my new tattoo, most of my wounds were already healing, but there were a few that would take a bit longer. Michael had really given me a beating.

“Why are you telling me this?” I asked.

“The Council sent me to strip you, but I don’t think you deserve to be sent to oblivion.”

“Strip me? How?”

“Your ring. Take it off and you lose your wings. Smear the stone with your blood and your soul will be imprisoned for eternity. At least until I decide to release you, or destroy you.”

“Destroy me? Angels can’t die.”

“That’s what the Council would have you believe,” Michael said.

“I don’t suppose you’re going to tell me how you’d do that?”

Michael’s shoulders shook as he laughed. “Not a chance in Hell.”

I sniggered and narrowed my eyes. I had time, and I’d get the answer some day.

“Why are you letting me go? Won’t you get in trouble?” I asked.

“I can sweet-talk the Council. Besides, every time you look at that tattoo, you’ll remember who you defied and what you left behind. Being on Earth marked with a permanent reminder of what you did is a far better punishment."

When Michael put it that way, suddenly oblivion seemed like the better option. "Eternity, huh?" I spun the ring on my finger and stared at the black stone. "Would I know what was happening?"

"Your soul would suffer a constant feeling of loss and hopelessness."

"Well," I scoffed, "that wouldn't be much different to how I feel right now."

"There is one difference," Michael said. "You wouldn't feel pain."

"No pain." I laughed. "Then maybe I should do it myself." I slowly slid the ring down my finger to the first knuckle.

Michael shook his head. "It wouldn't make a difference. All you'd do is strip yourself. You can't imprison your soul in your own ring."

"Then do it!" I thrust my hand at Michael.

"No, I don't think I will." He folded his arms over his chest. "Like I said, this is far better. And I'll have fun watching."

"Where are we anyway?" I asked.

"In a little Australian country town called Hopetown Valley. Grace will be here soon, too."

My fists clenched. "What! I did this to get away from her. And now you're telling me she'll be here soon. How long?"

"We both know time moves differently down here. Minutes in Heaven—or Hell—are potentially years on Earth. Time is irrelevant to us."

"How. Long!" I shoved Michael.

He shook his head. "You know how it works. Information is sacred. We're only told what we need to know."

"Please, don't hold out on me. I have to know."

"The Council is going to send her on an indefinite mission. That's all I can say. It's bad enough I've brought you here. The rest is up to you."

Michael offered me his hand. I found it hard to believe after all we'd been through he still wanted to try and part on good terms. I wasn't as willing.

"No. We're not friends, Michael. We never have been," I said.

He lowered his hand. "I'll see you around. You know this is far from over."

I knew.

I waited until Michael disappeared into the trees before taking my eyes off his back and getting a good look at my surroundings. I couldn't stay. If Grace was going to show up soon, I didn't want to be there when she did. Finding her was something I wanted to do on my own terms, not Michael's. One day I *would* find Grace, and I'd torture myself over her until it almost killed me, because that was what I deserved. I should never have done what I did, but I'd made my bed, and I'd lie in it until the end.

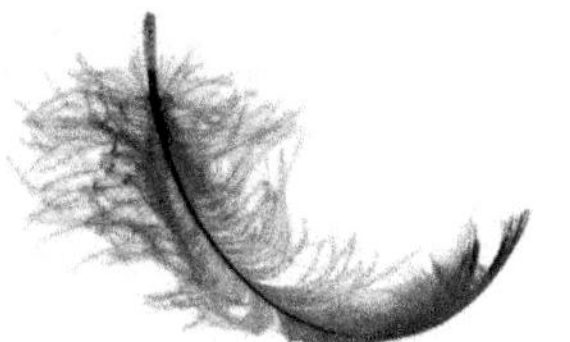

PART TWO
GRACE

7

One minute I was grabbing for him, the next he was gone. Seth had just renounced his God, and I was completely alone.

I hovered in the darkness, my wings beating gently, and I stared at the diamond that lay in my palm. What did it mean? He'd shed a tear for me. He was obviously upset, but why did he leave? My fingers curled around the diamond and I closed my hand into a tight fist. My body shook and I sobbed loudly. Tears filled my eyes and the stars blurred, forming streaks of light across the darkness.

How could I go home without him?

I wrapped my arms around myself and tried to hold it together. My heart was breaking into a thousand tiny pieces, and I was scared they would spill from my chest and scatter across the galaxy. Suddenly, I was nothing but a tiny speck in an enormous void of space, surrounded

59

by sadness. I needed to know where he'd gone, but I didn't know where to start looking. I had to return home.

I wiped the tears from my eyes and searched the darkness of the outer realm until I pinpointed the re-entry star. I flew towards it with heavy wings. It swallowed me and I was once again floating on cloud dust.

When I re-entered the departure level, I fell to my knees. The dust billowed around me and engulfed me in whiteness. I vaguely heard a voice speaking, but it seemed so far away. It wasn't until Daniel lifted me from the floor that I heard what he was saying.

"What happened, Grace?" His strong arms held me and I leant against his chest.

All I could do was shake my head. I couldn't speak; I had no words to express my feeling of loss.

Daniel began to run. Through blurry eyes I watched over his shoulder as he left a trail through the cloud dust. It looked pretty, the way it floated in the air then settled back into place. He raced up the spiral staircase then orbed on the run. We landed in the centre of the cloud field.

Daniel gently set me on my feet but kept a firm hold around my waist. I was grateful because if he'd let go I'd have crumpled to the floor.

From beside me I heard Angelica's voice amidst several others, and then I couldn't breathe. There were too many angels around me, closing in and suffocating me. I bowed my head and covered my face with my hands.

A tirade of comments and questions passed between the angels. What happened? Where's Seth? Why didn't he come home with you? It was too much. All my anger and pain bubbled inside me. It rose up and threatened to unleash itself. But I didn't let it break through; I wouldn't. Instead, I suppressed it and withdrew inside myself where it was quiet and no one could touch me.

The floor beneath my feet shook, and the angels around me scattered.

"Leave her alone," Michael boomed across the field.

When the cloud dust settled I raised my head and watched him walk over to Daniel and me. His brow creased into a frown. I probed his mind for answers, but because Michael was an archangel I didn't get much. His guard was a lot stronger than mine. Although, there was one thing I saw that slashed my already broken heart to ribbons.

"You knew," I whispered. We stood in silence for only a few moments, but it seemed like an infinite amount of time. "You knew!" I shouted this time. I broke free of Daniel's grasp and hit Michael in the chest with all the force I could muster. "Why did you let him do this? How could you let him leave? Why?" I pounded my fists on his chest until they were sore.

Michael stood and took everything I dished out. He didn't move and his expression didn't waver. When my energy waned he gently held my wrists to make me stop. I looked up into his milk chocolate eyes and I couldn't hold it in any longer. All the pain and hurt came rushing out of my mouth in a cry so guttural I feared my soul would pour out with it.

"It was his decision, Grace. Believe me when I say I tried to stop him," Michael said.

"Well, you didn't try hard enough." I took a deep breath and my whole body shook. "I'll never forgive him for this. Never."

"Forgiveness is the first step to healing."

"No." I shook my head. "He's my best friend, and he left with no explanation. He doesn't deserve my forgiveness."

The faces of thousands of angels stared at me in sympathy. Angelica came over and took my hand. She'd never gotten along very well with Seth, but they had tolerated each other because of me. She pursed her lips into a forced smile and squeezed my hand.

In time you'll forget the pain, she said. *You're better off without him. He obviously didn't care enough about you to stay, and he wasn't a true servant of God.*

How can you say that? He's my best friend, and I don't think I'll ever forget the pain. I slipped my hand from hers and walked away, focussing on the cloud field gates.

He was *your best friend,* Angelica shot back.

I ignored her. All I wanted was to get away from the stares and sympathetic expressions. I needed space and time to grieve. Actually, I needed my best friend back, but there was no returning from where Seth had gone.

Everything happens for a reason, Angelica said.

Some things shouldn't happen, I replied.

"Just leave her be," Michael said.

When I reached the gate I brushed it with my fingers and it opened silently for me. The cloud dust stirred and I leant down to run my fingers through it, concentrating on its texture to distract myself. It was like warm mist, but it wasn't wet.

I let my feet carry me wherever they wanted. My heart twinged as I remembered how Seth used to walk every-where. I'd always thought it was a waste of time. Why walk when you could orb or fly and be where you wanted to be in seconds? I was beginning to understand the walking. There was more time to take everything in, like the way the brilliance of Heaven danced around me as I passed through it.

For the first time I took a good look at my surroundings. I'd always taken my place in Heaven for granted, and I realised there were so many things I'd been taking for granted: the other angels around me, my friends, my family, my place in the scheme of things. We are often unaware of what we have until it's taken away from us.

In Heaven we all lived in unison, but there were places to go if we wanted to be alone. My feet carried me to the lowest level—the reflection level. It was there that I stayed for an indefinable amount of time. In Heaven time passed differently. It was as if there was no time.

I lay on my stomach and coaxed the clouds apart with my hands. But no matter how hard I tried, I couldn't find him. I believed Seth either no longer existed, or he was somewhere I couldn't see. Even though he'd hurt me, I prayed he was safe, knowing my prayer would go unanswered. Why would my Father watch over one of the fallen?

I rolled onto my back and stretched my arms out from my sides. Slowly, I moved them back and forth. The feeling of the soft mist against my skin calmed me, and I closed my eyes. When I opened them, Angelica stood over me.

I stared up into her pale denim eyes. She didn't say anything; she just lay down beside me and began to move her own arms in time with mine.

"Feels nice, doesn't it," I said after a while.

"I've never done this before," Angelica replied.

"I love running my hands through the cloud dust."

"Hmm, I think I'll have to do it more often."

We made cloud dust angels until our arms grew tired. Eventually I sat up, drew my knees to my chest, and wrapped my wings around my shoulders.

"I haven't been able to find him," I said.

Angelica sat up as well and faced me. Her wings shivered and the way the light played on their pearly surface mesmerised me.

"I don't think you'll be able to," she said. "We can't see the fallen from here."

"I need to know where he is," I whispered. "To see him with my own eyes."

"You need to forget about him. He left and there's nothing you can do." Angelica hesitated. "I'm sorry, I know it's harsh, but you have to forget about him, Grace. If he cared about you he would never have left. By leaving he's shown you he doesn't care one damn bit. He never cared about you. If he did, he'd have stayed. No angel would give up their place in Heaven if they weren't evil."

"He's not evil," I said. "You don't know him like I do."

"Did you know him well enough to see he'd do this? That he'd leave his best friend? No, Grace, you're wrong." Angelica shook her head. "He is evil, and the sooner you lock him out of your heart, the better."

"I just … I don't understand," I whispered.

"Come on, everyone's been waiting for you to come back to the cloud field. You've been gone so long."

"Maybe I need another mission to take my mind off things."

"I think that's a great idea." Angelica got to her feet

and stretched her hand down to me. I grabbed it and she pulled me up. "Hopefully, if you come back with me, the Council will give you one. But you have to promise me one thing. When you walk through that gate up there you leave all this behind. You have to forget about Seth."

Could I do that? I wasn't sure if I could forget my best friend and what he did to me; it hurt too much. How do you forget pain that intense? How do you block it out so it doesn't exist? But if I wanted to get myself back on track, I would have to do it. I'd have to suppress everything and get on with my duties. I had to convince myself Seth was completely gone. He was dead to me. There was no other way.

"I promise," I said. At least keeping promises was something I was good at.

8

Thousands of angels orbed and walked around the various levels of Heaven on their way to whatever mission or duty they needed to perform. Angelica walked with me back to the cloud field gates. She never questioned why I wanted to walk, and it was nice to have someone to walk with. I regretted not walking with Seth more, but quickly squashed the thought down into the depths of my heart where I'd locked away all the pain.

The gate shimmered as I neared. I heard it whisper a welcome before I stroked it with my fingers and it opened. My re-entrance to the field was a little unnerving. So many faces stared at me. I should have been at ease amongst my friends and family, but when you've had the angel's equivalent of a nervous breakdown, you become a little more sceptical.

Everyone smiled and nodded as I passed them, then

went back to whatever conversations they'd been engrossed in. Angelica stayed by my side until I found my usual place. I stared at the patch of cloud dust that looked like every other part of the field, but at the same time it didn't. With Seth gone I couldn't sit there. That spot had heard many conversations and watched our friendship grow over time. But everything had changed. I walked a little further before settling down.

"Are you all right?" Angelica asked.

"Just peachy," I replied. Angelica raised her eyebrows. "And you have no idea how grateful I'll be when I see Michael."

I never thought I'd want to see the archangel again—he knew what Seth had planned to do, and he didn't stop him—but he was my ticket out and back to Earth. If I wasn't summoned, I wasn't going anywhere in a hurry. He must have heard me and was playing games, because he took his time coming. With every passing moment I grew more and more frustrated, until I got to my feet and went to the centre of the field.

"Michael," I called. The other angels stopped what they were doing to watch, but I didn't care. I held my arms away from my sides and tilted my head back. "Michael!" I yelled this time. "I'm ready. Would you get your butt down here?"

The cloud dust in front of me exploded and it funnelled upwards like a water spout. It settled back into place and Michael stared at me, his arms folded over his chest.

"Do you ever grow tired of showing up like that?" I asked.

He laughed. "No way. It's fun, and you'd expect nothing less."

That was true. The day Michael didn't explode cloud dust I'd be surprised.

"Are you here because I called you, or because they need me?"

"That depends which answer you want."

I stared at Michael and furrowed my brow. "I think you know which answer I want. I have to get out of here. I need another mission."

I'm not sure if that's a good idea. Michael relaxed his arms to his sides. *Walk with me.*

I fell into step beside Michael and he took us away from the other angels to a part of the field that was quiet. He dipped his hand in the cloud dust and moulded it until there were two forms resembling chairs. He gestured for me to sit before lowering himself to his seat. Michael hitched his white pants and rested his elbows on his knees. His hands hung loosely clasped between them.

I sighed. "Come on, out with it."

"The Council have summoned you, but I'm not entirely sure if it's for a normal mission, I don't want you to get your hopes up," he said. "They seem to think you're rather fragile."

"Can you blame me? I've lost my best friend."

"Seth is not the first angel to fall."

"But he's the first that shouldn't have. He is good, and kind. I know he is. What reason could he possibly have for doing what he did?"

Michael hesitated. "I can't answer that."

"Well, I can't stay here. It's killing me," I said. "I need a distraction." I met Michael's friendly, brown eyes and wished he wasn't so nice. I was still angry with him for not telling me about Seth's intentions. "Why didn't you tell me what he was planning to do? You should have stopped him."

"It wasn't my place to tell, Grace. You should know our word is solid and means a great deal. I gave Seth my word. And yes, I could have stopped him, but he made a decision and I actually respect it."

I closed my eyes and rubbed them with the heels of my hands. "You know I'm mad at you, don't you?"

"I know, but I also know you'll forgive me." Michael stood and offered me his hand. I took it. He gently pulled me to my feet and embraced me in a brotherly hug. "Whatever you decide, Grace, make sure your decisions are true to what you believe to be right. Now go. The Council is waiting."

I left the cloud field and turned Michael's words over in my mind. I always tried to do what was right. I hoped it would be enough.

The journey to the Council's chamber was peaceful, and I couldn't remember the last time I'd actually walked there. Usually, I orbed myself straight to the door. I watched the staircase disappear into the clouds behind me as I climbed each step. I marvelled at the feeling of wading through the waist-high dust to get to the chamber door.

My palm tingled with warmth when I pressed it to the marble slab. It slid open silently and I went straight to the centre of the room where I waited for the Council to speak. It seemed like they took forever.

"Grace," they finally said. Their combined voice resonated around the chamber. "What are we to do with you? Are you ready to return to full service?"

"I will go wherever you want me to go."

"Did your time on the lower level help you recover from your situation?" the Council asked.

I hesitated. "I don't think I'll ever fully recover. But I think time away will help me forget."

The chamber fell silent. I wrung my hands together, waiting in anticipation for them to speak again.

"We've been watching you over the past couple of centuries, and it is evident to us that you would probably do more good by serving on another mission."

"Thank you!" I exclaimed.

"Please, let us finish."

I mumbled sorry under my breath and waited for them to continue.

"This mission is not one to enter into lightly. You must understand it is a great commitment that requires your complete devotion."

I didn't quite understand why they'd said that. Every mission I'd ever been on required my complete devotion; that's what it was all about. The clouds parted and the floor of the chamber opened up. It revealed the image of a young woman and her husband seated at a table. The woman rose and placed a hand on her pregnant belly. A sense of déjà vu washed over me. *Another pregnant woman,* I thought.

"Am I saving her or the baby this time?" I asked.

"Neither," the Council said.

I was confused. "Her husband then?" I waited for the silence to be filled with the Council's answer.

"This couple are the first in what we hope will be a long lineage. The woman is carrying twins who will be born to serve a very specific purpose."

"So, I am saving the babies?"

"Grace," the Council sighed, and it sounded like a collection of different pitched voices. A mound in the cloud dust formed beside me. "Sit. And just listen."

I sat.

"The situation in Australia is becoming dire," the Council continued. My ears pricked at the mention of a country other than England. This was going to be good. "And we need to set something in place to alleviate it. The birth of these twins is vital in the fight against evil, and their role is important. The boy will be born first. He is the hunter. He is human but stronger, faster, and more agile—built specifically to fight the ultimate creature of evil. The vampire."

"You're creating a vampire hunter?" I asked.

"The girl," the Council went on, ignoring my question, "is the protector. She will also hunt, but her main duty is to protect her brother. We already have some teams like this stationed at various places around the world. One particular linage in England is still alive and strong, thanks to the efforts of your last mission. But a need has arisen for another location to be protected. Hopetown Valley is under vampire attack. The creatures are moving from the cities into the country areas in search of more secluded feeding grounds."

"The twins Seth and I saved grew up to be vampire hunters?" I asked. "But I don't understand. What part will I play in this if I don't need to ensure the safety of these unborn children?"

"You will *be* one of these children."

I needed to sit down, but I was already sitting down.

The silence in the chamber was thick. I tried to let the Council's last words sink in, but they bounced off me and spiralled out of control around the circular room.

"Um, can you repeat that, please?" I eventually said.

"The children you saved on your last mission: one was a Protection Angel—like you will be—and the other was a hunter. The man sitting at that table is distantly related to William."

The face of the baby boy Seth and I saved came to the front of my mind. I watched the man in the image below me and tried to see if there was any resemblance. He smiled at his wife as she set a cup on the table in front of him. He pulled her onto his lap and gave her an affectionate cuddle, kissing her belly. I still couldn't quite fathom what the Council was asking of me.

"We've specifically chosen this couple to be your parents. Their names are John and Sophia Tate. They know what is expected of them, and that you will be special. You will be born into this generation of hunters, to grow alongside your brother and keep him true to his path. You will protect him until he is ready to be trained, and you will keep protecting him until it is time to be born into the next generation."

Again I had to let the information sink in. I'd never in my existence been asked to undertake a mission as complicated as this. Usually we went to Earth, saved someone important or prevented a tragedy, then came home. This was something different entirely: an indefinite mission. The Council said there were already other Protection Angels out there. It was possible. There were so many of us there was no way I could know all the angels that lived in Heaven, or all those currently serving on Earth.

"I'm not sure I fully understand how this will work. I'll be re-born, over and over?" I asked. "Why? Why not stay and protect each son when he's born?"

The Council sighed. "You need to form a bond with each generation, and we feel the best way to do that is in utero. You will be completely in tune with each other; thinking and acting together when needed."

"But what about the down time? Our younger years, and the time we need to train?" I had so many questions the Council would not be happy about. The air in the room tightened with their frustration, but if they wanted me to do this, I needed to know the details.

"Grace, we've never known an angel to ask as many questions as you."

"How do you get any answers if you don't ask questions?" I said.

The Council remained silent for a few moments before continuing. "Very well. Your parents will continue the fight while you are young and in training; specifically your father. He is the one that keeps the lineage going. Your mother will learn skills as your father trains your new brother, but her main role is to nurture you both in your younger years."

"Um, so basically my brother will become my dad? That's just weird. And yucky."

Another collective sigh. "Your soul is divine. You are not related to them by blood."

"It's still yucky," I mumbled.

"Is there anything else you would like to know before

you leave?" the Council asked.

"Yes, one more question. What happens to me when it's time to be born again? Do I just vanish into thin air? Won't people ask questions?"

"Each generation will be treated differently and dealt with when the time comes. You will know when it's time to move on."

"Will I know what's happening?" I asked. "When I'm ... born."

"What happened to one more question?" The Council made a noise that I could only describe as chuckling. "You will know everything from the moment you are inside your mother. You need to in order to do your job."

"Ok, ok, ok," I breathed. "This is really weird. You want me to become a baby then grow up beside a human who will be my twin brother and protect him while we fight vampires? Then I'll die and be re-born to do it all over again? Several times?"

The Council remained silent. I stood and ran my hands through my hair. The couple below me continued to smile and laugh happily with each other. It would be strange, being inside someone's belly, then going through childhood and actually growing as a human would do. Angels aren't born; we are created, and I don't remember my creation. I just remember being there and receiving my creation ring.

"Will I keep my powers?"

"You will be able to do everything you can do now. It will be the same as every other time you've been sent to Earth," the Council replied.

"How long is this mission?" I asked.

"The determined amount of time is indefinite. You will

serve until such time as we see fit. Or a time when you are no longer needed to carry out your duty."

"Then it's pretty much forever?"

"We are not asking for you to agree, Grace. We are asking you to comply," the Council said.

"Yeah, I know. What you say goes." I watched the cloud dust float over the image of the couple until they were completely obscured. "When do I leave? Can I say goodbye to everyone?"

The marble door appeared in the wall of the chamber and I took it as my answer. What would I say to my friends, to all the angels that had been my family for so many years? I'd been selfish in my grief over the loss of Seth; he'd been their friend and brother, too. They'd lost him as well, and now they would lose me. Maybe not in quite the same way, but I didn't know when I'd be back. I might never come back.

My body went numb as my feet carried me to the chamber door. It slid open at my touch and I stepped across the threshold.

The Council spoke one last time, their voice echoing off the chamber walls. "Good luck, Grace. We'll see you in your dreams."

9

The silence was eerie as I entered the cloud field. It was as if everyone knew I had news, and they were holding their breaths waiting for me to speak. How was I going to tell them I was leaving? Thankfully, before I had to, Michael made one of his showy entrances.

He held my gaze with his serious brown eyes. There was something in his stare that unsettled me. I gently probed his mind for an answer. Surprisingly, he let me in—but only so far.

No details, Grace. Just know he isn't in Hell.

For now, that would have to be enough.

Why did he do it? I asked. *You know, don't you?*

As much as I want to, I can't tell you. Michael blinked. He shoved me out of his mind, startling me.

"I'll never forgive him."

"Never is a long time," Michael said.

Angelica floated over and laid a gentle hand on my arm. "You're going on another mission, aren't you?"

"I have to; everything here reminds me of him. Leaving is the only way I'll be able to forget," I said. "And I don't know how long I'll be gone."

"Yes, but unlike Seth, you'll come back eventually," Angelica said. "He's a traitor and a coward, and I hope he gets what he deserves."

I frowned at her. "If this is your way of helping me forget about him, it's not working."

"Grace, I—"

"No. Don't keep talking, Angelica. For once just keep your mouth shut."

The angels surrounded me, offering hugs and words of encouragement. Angelica got pushed to the outer edge but moved with us as the crowd swept me along to the earth-bound gate. I'd lost sight of Michael and when I finally managed to look back at him, he stood in the middle of the field with his arms folded.

Goodbye, I said. *Thanks for being a great arch, even if you are annoying.*

This isn't goodbye, Grace. We'll see each other again. Just make sure you're prepared for anything.

Always pack my toothbrush? I giggled.

Something like that, yes. Michael smiled and it filled the field with light. It was the last thing I saw before the gate closed and I had nowhere else to go but the departure pad.

10

Daniel smiled warmly when I approached the departure desk.

"You know, I think I've lost count of how many times I've sent you down to Earth," he said.

"Really?" I asked. "Because I can remember every single one of my missions."

"I know. I was only joking." Daniel's expression grew serious. He stared at me for a long time. Finally, he spoke again. "This is the first time on your own, though."

"I guess it is. I hadn't really thought about it." I stared at my hands and fiddled with my ring. Why did Daniel have to point out that Seth wasn't with me? Sadness overwhelmed me, and for a moment all I wanted was to sink into the surrounding mist and disappear. I wanted it to swallow me up and encase me in warmth, to shut everything else out.

"I'm going to miss you," Daniel said.

I looked up into his open face and struggled to hold back the tears that threatened to spill onto my cheeks.

"We'll see each other again."

"I know." He handed me the clipboard. "I just get all mushy when an angel is sent on an indefinite."

I signed the sheet and handed the clipboard back to Daniel. He set it on the desk then came around to join me on the other side.

"It's going to be different this time. You won't really land anywhere," he said.

I took a deep breath and let it out slowly. The dust on the departure pad began to swirl; that was my cue. My stomach tightened with nerves and I wrung my hands together.

"Thanks, for everything," I said.

Daniel gave me an awkward hug and patted me on the back. "This isn't goodbye. You'll return someday, and I'll still be here."

The comfort from Daniel's embrace lingered around me as I stepped onto the departure pad. I turned to face him, smiled, and gave a small wave.

"You'll be fine, Grace. I haven't seen you fail a mission yet."

Daniel's reassuring voice was the last thing I heard as everything turned white.

11

1874

When I opened my eyes I was greeted by darkness. My body floated inside a warm bubble, and the steady rhythm of a heartbeat pulsed around me. I heard the sound of muffled voices. When I reached out my hands I touched someone. Instantly, I realised it was my brother. A thin membrane separated us, but I could still feel his emotions and hear his thoughts.

Don't be scared, I said. *I'm here to protect you.*

There was a squeeze. Gentle pressure pushed our bodies closer, and for a moment we jostled for position in the cramped space.

Someone cried out in pain.

Here we go, I said. *It's your turn first. I'll meet you on the other side.*

12

1889
First Incarnation – Fifteen Years Old

The horses brayed and tossed their heads as my father adjusted the buggy pole. It was my favourite day of the week. Mother and Father were going into town for supplies, and that meant my brother and I had the whole day to do as we pleased.

"I trust you two will stay out of trouble," Father said. My brother, Samuel, grunted in reply from his seat on the cottage steps.

"Of course they will," Mother said. "They never get into any trouble they can't handle." She winked at me and ruffled Samuel's hair on her way past.

"We'll see you later this afternoon." Father held Mother's hand and helped her into the buggy. He flicked the reins and the horses pulled them off down the long drive.

I walked away from the house to the centre of the clearing and turned my face to the sun. Samuel came to stand with me and we went through our little ritual, like we did every town day. We stood back to back. At six-foot-two, he was an entire foot taller than me, so the back of my head fit comfortably into the curve of his neck. We entwined our fingers and I closed my eyes. Slowly, we raised our arms out to the side and Samuel bent forward. I leant back into him and waited for the exact moment to flick my legs into the air. Once I was up, I balanced on his back for a few minutes.

It was an odd ritual, but it reinforced our trust in each other. I trusted Samuel completely. For fifteen years I'd protected him, shadowed him wherever he went. We shared an unbreakable bond, even if we had a funny way of showing it.

A sound in the forest startled me and I fell. Before I hit the ground I orbed and landed on my feet in front of Samuel. He stumbled forward but managed to stop himself crashing into me.

"What was that?" I whipped my head around in an attempt to find out where the sound had come from. "Someone is in the forest."

"I don't see anyone," Samuel said.

Something flashed through the trees. It was almost white and gleamed in the dull forest light. I focused on it and orbed. When I landed all I saw was a cloud of dissipating black mist.

"Grace, what's going on?" Samuel joined me amongst the trees.

"There was someone right here," I said.

"I think maybe you're—"

I saw the flash again and orbed before Samuel could finish his sentence.

"Crazy," I mumbled to myself when I landed.

The mist I'd seen the first time swirled in front of me before dissipating into nothing. I was a bit baffled. I'd never seen someone disappear in a cloud of mist before. I'd seen plenty of vampires explode into dust, but never black mist. I walked back to the clearing where Samuel sat on the grass waiting.

"Are you finished being crazy?" he asked.

I flopped down across from him and picked at a tuft of grass. "I think someone is watching us," I whispered. "You know how careful we have to be."

"I know," Samuel sighed. Then he used our twin connection and spoke in my head. *Are you going to launch into your "We're here to save the world" speech again?*

I pursed my lips, and brushed the dirt and bits of grass from my hands.

"This is serious," I hissed, smacking him on the arm. *No one can know what we do. And if there is someone watching us, it can't be good.*

Samuel leant back on his hands and stretched his legs out beside me. "Don't worry about it; we're vampire hunters, who could possibly be watching us that we can't handle?"

"Shhh!" I smacked him again. "Keep your voice down. We don't know who's out there."

Well, it's not a vamp; it's the middle of the day, Samuel said silently.

Then he froze.

His eyes searched for something over my head and he furrowed his brow. *Don't look,* he said before I had the chance to turn around. *I'll show you. Just pretend we're still talking.*

I stalled; then started talking a little too eagerly. "What do you want to do today?" I asked. I chattered about anything I could think of while Samuel showed me what he was looking at. All he had to do was hold the image in his mind and I could go in and take a peek.

You're right, Samuel said. *Someone is watching us.*

A figure stood in the forest beneath the shadow of the trees. It stepped forward and my breath caught in my throat. I had to force myself to keep talking. Samuel was responding but I didn't hear the words coming from his mouth. His mind held the image of a face I hadn't seen in a long time. A face I'd struggled to push out of my thoughts and my heart. After all the time that had passed, he hadn't changed. His eyes still wore the same hardened and pained expression they'd held when I'd last looked into them.

"Seth," I breathed. But when I turned to look, he was gone.

13

1947
Third Incarnation – Twenty Years Old

The vampire growled and lunged at me. I orbed and landed behind him, then staked him in the back before he had the chance to figure out where I'd gone. My brother, Robert, had lost his stake and was fighting another vamp hand to hand. She'd been pretty, but Robert could pack a mean punch and her face was bleeding too much to be sexy. Unfortunately, punching a vampire wouldn't kill it. I orbed again and drove my stake into her back. She fell to the forest floor in a heap of dust and I faced my brother.

"You make it look so easy," Robert said. He bent and put his hands on his knees to catch his breath.

"You would, too, if you could orb."

"Yes, quite an unfair advantage." Robert straightened up and followed me deeper into the forest.

We were on our nightly hunt and only just getting started. I was hoping we wouldn't be too busy. There was something I needed to talk to Robert about, but it wasn't going to be easy. I'd been by his side for twenty years, and it was almost time for the next generation to come through. The first two times I had to have *the talk* with my brother, we'd been a few years older. This time it had come earlier than I'd expected. Robert had a girlfriend he'd been with for almost a year. He didn't know she'd been selected by the Council to be the next Tate wife. When the Council gave clearance, I had one, maybe two, years before it was time to start again.

We walked for a while with nothing but the forest sounds for company. The night was clear and the stars flickered through the canopy above. I was about to say something when I sensed someone in the forest. Robert did as well and we both stopped to listen. After a few moments I sighed and cursed under my breath.

"Would you just come out," I called into the darkness. "We know you're there."

A shadow emerged from the trees. "It's a nice night for a walk."

"What do you want, Seth?" Robert asked.

Robert didn't know anything about my history with the fallen angel that followed us around like a bad smell. None of my brothers had. It wasn't something I wanted to talk about. I just gritted my teeth, clenched my fists and took his presence like a hot poker in my eye. I survived on the fact he'd eventually go away.

"Just checking up on Grace." Seth's mouth curled at the corners but I didn't stick around long enough to see him smile. I walked back the way we'd come. "One day you'll talk to me," Seth called.

"No chance," I yelled over my shoulder.

It wasn't until Robert had caught up to me I realised I was almost running. "Hey, slow down." He grabbed my arm. "He's gone."

I slowed to a walk and fell into step with Robert. He knew not to ask questions about Seth. We'd been down that steep and rocky road before, and it always ended with me yelling. I couldn't blame Robert for wanting to know about my past, but as far as I was concerned it was none of his business.

"So…" I eventually said. "There's something we need to discuss."

Robert chuckled. "I was wondering when you were going to start *the talk*."

"You can feel it, too?"

"I've always known we wouldn't be doing this together forever—must be something in my DNA." Robert stopped and leant against a tallowwood.

"Yes, you're special. We both are. But you already know that."

"Then tell me what I don't know," he said.

I sat nearby on a fallen log and launched into an explanation of our expected future. Robert listened intently as I explained the mechanics of it all. How his girlfriend, Adele, had already been selected by the Council. That when she fell pregnant it would be time for me to leave, but we still had at least a year together.

"What will happen to you?" he asked.

"My body will die and be buried in the family cemetery." Robert raised his eyebrows. "It's further into the forest, but only someone with Tate blood can find it. It's protected by an enchantment."

"Do you ... die the same way every time?"

"It won't be violent if that's what you're worried about. The first time I died at home. Then with Dad, he told everyone there'd been an accident. No one asked questions. Hopetown Valley is a small, country town—accidents aren't uncommon."

"And this time around?"

"We won't know until it comes," I said. "You'll see me again."

Robert dropped his gaze and rubbed his face with his hand. "I know, but it's still sad. It's hard to come to terms with the knowledge I'll lose my sister soon."

"I'll be back. You'll be busy fighting, and before you know it, you'll be training my next brother." Leaves rustled in the forest and I smiled. "You can come out now, Dad."

Robert chuckled as Dad stepped out from behind a tree. Moonlight shone in his eyes and he shook his head. "You're good, Grace."

"And you're getting careless in your old age."

"Come on." Dad clapped Robert on the back. "Enough for tonight. Your grandfather is asking after you."

We headed towards home. Dad walked with his arm draped over Robert's shoulders. The way they interacted made me smile, and my heart lurched at the thought of leaving. Every time it got harder, even though I knew I'd see both of them again.

My skin prickled and I sensed a presence. I knew Seth had returned, and for the second time that night I wished he'd leave me alone.

"I'll catch up to you in a minute," I said to Dad and Robert.

Dad turned and scanned the trees. He could sense Seth as well, and his face tightened into a frown. "Don't stay out too much longer," he finally said

"I won't."

I slowed my pace until Robert and Dad were almost out of sight along the forest path; then I stopped.

"What is your problem?" I said, staring into the trees.

Seth stepped into view and folded his arms over his chest. I stopped and actually looked at him. He hadn't changed much. He still had the attitude and the swagger; he just seemed harder around the edges somehow. His almost black eyes stared me down, and there was something in them that frightened me.

"Nice tattoo," I said, dragging my eyes from his and staring at his left forearm.

"Battle scar. I blame Michael."

"I hope it hurt."

"Why won't you talk to me?" he asked. "Why do you keep running?"

My mouth dropped open. "Are you serious? I can't believe you're even asking me that." I shook my head. The forest talked in whispers as a breeze wove its way through the trees. My hair flicked into my eyes and I batted it away in frustration. "A long time ago I made a promise to myself that I'd forget about you. You're dead to me."

Seth flinched. "Can we please talk about this?"

"Oh, *now* you want to talk! What's there to talk about? You want to know why I keep running away from you? Why I can't stand the sight of you?" I raced towards Seth and shoved him as hard as I could. He stumbled backwards, tripped on a tree root and landed on his butt. "Because you left—with no explanation. You ripped my heart out and you left. So you don't get the privilege of talking to me."

"Then why are you still standing here?" Seth looked up and I met his cold stare.

I turned and walked away, and I didn't look back.

14

The crisp morning air hit my face as I opened the door to the shed. Dew sparkled on the grass in the clearing, converting it to a field of diamonds.

It was the best time of day, but at this early hour, Archer and Pa were still fast asleep. For me, the morning represented a new beginning. The day was yet to unfold, and I could make it whatever I wanted it to be. I'd been searching for a new beginning a lot lately.

This time around, everything had been harder. Three years ago we'd unexpectedly lost our parents. But I guess when you fight vampires for a living, there's bound to be some casualties. I hadn't expected it to be Mum and Dad.

Mum knew how to fight, but she wasn't a fighter. Her

job was the same in every generation: to raise us, and keep my brother grounded in this insane world. Even the best hunter wouldn't have stood a chance, and I'm yet to find out who was responsible for their deaths. One day I will, and I'll make them pay.

For the first time we'd been without our most important hunter. It was also the first time Dad wasn't there to train my brother. In less than a week, Archer would begin his training. Pa really had his work cut out for him. He was an excellent hunter, but he wasn't getting any younger.

I walked into the forest and took the path I'd taken so many times before. I followed it until I reached a place where the bracken fern didn't grow. Just off the path was a nice flat rock, perfect for sitting on. Before I had the chance to get comfortable in one of my favourite spots, the leaves on the forest floor rustled and a boy stepped out from behind the trees.

His appearance shocked me into silence. Through each of my incarnations I'd looked different, but the imprint of my soul never changed. This time around I'd chosen to be my true self. How I was when I'd been in Heaven. I had the same messy mop of wild black hair, pale ivory skin, and just a hint of rose in my cheeks.

Instantly, I knew who the boy was even though I'd never seen him so young. He'd always looked the same: tanned skin, blond hair and dark, menacing eyes. This boy had all those features but seemed to be about my age. Usually angels—fallen or otherwise—didn't change their appearance. How this boy had shed his older self baffled me.

I was lost for words.

"Finally," he said. "You haven't run away yet."

The young version of Seth sat on the forest floor and crossed his legs. He picked up a leaf and crushed it in his hand, then let the broken pieces fall from his fingers.

"How..." I shook my head. "No. I don't want to know. I'll bet you made a deal with the devil."

Seth smirked. "Something like that."

"Did you sell your soul for your youth? Oh wait! You've already sold it."

Seth was silent for a few minutes. His dark eyes burned into me, but I refused to look away.

"Things will be different this time," he said. "I can grow up with you, instead of having to wait. Maybe then I can convince—"

"I don't want things to be different. I just want you to leave me alone."

I stood and headed for the path.

Seth chuckled, and he sounded like his older, truer self. "I can't do that, Grace. As much as I want to, I could never leave you alone."

"Then stay out of my way," I said.

"Or what?" he sniggered.

I orbed and landed behind Seth, grabbed him around the neck and pulled him to his feet. A ripple of shock course through me as my skin connected with his, and I realised it was the first time I'd been this close to him since he fell. Anger rose inside me and I shoved him as hard as I could. Seth lurched forward and sprawled onto his belly, gouging the dirt and scattering leaves in every direction. He rolled over and glared at me.

"Or I'll make you wish you'd never been created," I said.

Seth misted, and I let out a long breath. So much for my new beginning; I had a feeling it was going to be a bad day.

15

2003
Almost a week later

Archer sat beside me and stared at my hand as I twirled a twig between my fingers.

"You know, today's the day," I said.

"Yeah," he replied, raising his head to look into my eyes. "I know. I felt it coming."

The dry grass beneath me dug into my legs, and I turned my face skyward to the warmth of the midday sun. Tallowwood branches moved with the gentle breeze and cast dappled shadows around the edge of the clearing. Spring was turning to summer, and with it came the monotonous drone of the cicadas' song.

The large farm shed where we lived stood on one side of the clearing. Its shadow offered shelter from the heat.

It was tempting, but we both preferred the sunshine. Sweat trickled down my neck and I relished the feeling. I loved summer and everything about it. In my opinion it should be summer all year round, something our grandfather would never agree with.

"Are you two gonna sit there all day baking?" Pa's husky, but friendly voice floated across the clearing. "Come and help me for a minute, would you?"

We scrambled to our feet and ran to where Pa stood in the shade. He held out a large cane basket filled with the day's pickings and I grabbed it tightly by the handle.

"Easy there, Grace, she's heavy."

"It's ok, Pa, I got it."

"Be sure to clean them up good before you put them away."

"Sure thing, Pa," I said. I rested the basket on my foot and waited to see what else he had for us.

"Now you, young fella, have the biggest responsibility." Pa got down on one knee and handed Archer a smaller basket. "A good taking today—seven in total. Be sure not to smash them on your way across the clearing."

"Yes, Pa," Archer said quietly. He smiled up at Pa's big brown face. The same hazel eyes, flecked with gold, stared lovingly back at him.

"Make sure you come straight back," Pa said. "Today's the day."

We ran as fast as our loads would allow across to the shed. I rested the basket on my hip and flung the door open with my free hand. Archer dragged a milk crate over to the makeshift sink. I climbed up and busied myself washing the tomatoes and cleaning the other veggies. Archer took an egg carton from the old Kelvinator fridge and placed his loot into the empty spaces, careful not to break any.

"You know I'm not really your sister, don't you, Arch?"

He glanced over from where he'd sat down at the Formica kitchen table. His chin rested on his arm. "Sure, I know. I think I've always known."

"You know what today is, then?" I asked. I laid a tea towel on the bench and spread tomatoes across it.

"Yep. Today's the day I begin my training."

"Things will get harder from now on," I said. "You'll start to do and see things no one can know about. You have to be able to keep secrets."

"I'm not gonna tell anyone," he said. "Not ever."

I smiled, and my love for him glowed within me. He was my reason for existing. If it wasn't for him, and all my brothers before him, I'd still be in Heaven looking down on everything instead of experiencing it. But just like it was with every incarnation, my time with Archer wouldn't last forever. He would grow up—we both would—and the time would come when we'd have to say goodbye.

Archer followed me back to the clearing where Pa was waiting. Pa smiled warmly and motioned for us to follow him into the forest.

"Grace," Archer whispered. "Who is that?" He pointed into the trees.

I slipped my hand into his and gave it a gentle squeeze. "That's no one you need to worry about," I said.

The boy in the forest stood partially obscured by the trees, but I could still see his eyes. They locked onto mine as we walked past, and for a moment I let myself look at him.

One day, Grace, Seth said in my mind.

Not any time soon, I replied.

We'll see...

Pa called for us to hurry up and I looked ahead to where he was standing. When I glanced back at Seth there was nothing but a lingering cloud of black mist where he'd been.

"I'm scared, Gracie," Archer said, and it pulled my attention back to him.

"Don't be," I replied. I knew what was in store for Archer; I'd done it many times before, but he was understandably nervous. "You'll do great." I squeezed his hand again. "And just remember, I'll always be here to protect you."

THE TATE CHRONICLES

ACKNOWLEDGEMENTS

This time around the journey was a little easier, and I have several people to thank for that.

Brendon, again you have showed unwavering faith in me. Your support and love are my most treasured assets, thank you.

My wonderful children, you are the light that burns brightly in my dimly lit room. You never cease to amaze me, and I find your youthful ways inspiring. You have taught me how to laugh, and see the world through different eyes. Love you both.

Thank you to my parents for believing in me, and

encouraging me to follow my dreams. And thanks, Mum, for all your help with putting my commas in the right places.

Sacrifice wouldn't be what it is without the help of my critique partners and readers. Thank you to Stacey, Lauren, Cassandra, Emily M, and Sarah. I appreciate the time and effort you put into critiquing *Sacrifice,* and the valuable feedback you supplied.

Thank you to my Aussie Owned and Read girls: Stacey, Lauren, Cassandra, Katie, Suse, Sharon, and Emily JM. You have made me feel part of a wonderful family, and I'm immensely grateful for your ongoing support and encouragement.

Huge thanks to Katrina for being the one to read it first. Again you've let me subject you to numerous rounds of reading, and an endless number of emails. I value highly everything you do for me, and I'm grateful for your unconditional friendship and support. Thank you for being my alpha reader, spell checker, editor, and closest friend, all rolled into one.

And finally, thank you to my readers and followers for your amazing support. I've been lucky to have made some great friends along this journey. To everyone who has read *Fall For Me* and loved it, this one's for you.

ABOUT THE AUTHOR

K. A. Last was born in Subiaco, Western Australia, and moved to Sydney when she was eight. Artistic and creative by nature, she studied Graphic Design and graduated with an Advanced Diploma. After marrying her high school sweetheart, she concentrated on her career before settling into family life. Blessed with a vivid imagination, K. A. Last began writing to let off creative steam, and fell in love with it. She has a Bachelor of Arts Degree from Charles Sturt University, with a major in English, and minors in Children's Literature, Art History, and Visual Culture. She now resides in the NSW countryside with her family and a menagerie of animals.

CONNECT WITH
K. A. LAST

**Scan the code to subscribe
to K. A. Last's newsletter.**

Website www.kalastbooks.com.au
Facebook www.facebook.com/KALastBooks
Instagram www.instagram.com/kalastbooks
Pinterest www.pinterest.com/kalast
Goodreads www.goodreads.com/KALast
Twitter www.twitter.com/KALastBooks

BOOKS BY K. A. LAST

YA Fantasy Fiction
Sacrifice – A Fall For Me Prequel
Fall For Me (The Tate Chronicles, #1)
Fight For Me (The Tate Chronicles, #2)
Die For Me (The Tate Chronicles, #3)
Immagica
The Lovely Dark
Ella and Ash (Happily Ever After, #1)
Chasing Neve (Happily Ever After, #2)
False Princess (Happily Ever After, #3)
Dance of Wishes (Happily Ever After, #4)
Winter Flame (Happily Ever After, #5)

YA Contemporary Fiction
Something (All the Things: part one)
Nothing (All the Things: part two)
Everything (All the Things: part three)
The Other Side of Me (All the Things: part four)

Non-fiction
A Novel Idea! Colouring Journal for Writers
A Novel Idea Workbook for Writers